For

"You can always say,
'I knew her when...'"   ☺

Enjoy! Bobbi ♥

YOUNG TEACHER

Bobbi Ruggiero

Published by Scorpio Sister Press
Copyright 2016 Bobbi Ruggiero
All rights reserved.

No part of this publication may be reproduced, distributed, or transmitted
in any form or by any means, including photocopying, recording, or other
electronic or mechanical methods, without the prior written permission
of the author, except in the case of brief quotations embodied in critical
reviews.

This is a work of fiction. References to real people, places, organizations,
events or products are intended to provide a sense of authenticity and are
used fictitiously. All characters, incidents, and dialogue are drawn from
the author's imagination and not to be construed as real.

Totally awesome cover by Rosenbaum Creative

Young Teacher previously appeared in the 80s Mix Tape anthology
published by Pink Kayak Press, 2016

Dedicated to all the boys with guitars who make my knees weak.

And many thanks to everyone who believed I had a book in me. The list is long.

You know who you are. Smooches.

🎸 ONE

Julia

J ulia ate the same lunch three days a week.

Roasted turkey with cranberry sauce on whole wheat.

The same person made it for her on Monday, Wednesday and Friday.

Her Sandwich Guy.

Or Matthew, according to his nametag.

Matthew knew that she wanted only a smear of cranberry sauce. And to wrap it in paper, not the tinfoil that left a metallic taste on the bread. He'd hand it to her and she would allow herself to get lost in his blue-green eyes, his dimple, and shock of messy blonde hair underneath the goofy baseball cap he wore as part of his uniform. The edge of a colorful tattoo stuck out past the cuff of his shirtsleeve. Another, a small heart, on his right thumb. Recently, she began to wonder if those plump lips of his could kiss her well enough to make her knees weak. By the look of them, the answer was a resounding *yes*.

He didn't know her name and he'd been making her lunch for a while now. Did he even *want* to know it? He had stopped asking for her order and would simply smile at her and get to work when she showed up in his line.

She *always* got in his line.

She liked to watch him laugh with the other employees and swipe his hair off his face when the kitchen got busy and hot. And she really liked how his button-down shirt molded to his chest and long, lean back muscles. He moved his tall, lanky body with confidence and ease. Did he have a girlfriend? With his looks, he probably had more than one, and all at once. Every night. The thought made her insanely jealous.

Why?

She had a crush on him.

A crush that kept getting worse, especially after they started chatting a bit, mostly about music. Something was always playing in the shop, and she usually liked what she heard. Turned out they liked many of the same bands. She had toyed with giving him a list of songs she liked, just in case he wanted to check them out, but she didn't want to seem like some pathetic older woman trying to snag a young guy. In the fantasy, the young guy threw himself at *her*.

And Matthew was young. Like, *half her age* young.

"Listen, you are totally going out with me and Andrew tonight. There's this radical new singer and you will totally *love him*. He sounds like Sting. Please say yes. You never go out anymore."

Julia studied her planner, ignoring her assistant Kate's request, knowing it would drive her crazy. Kate hated to be ignored. Hated when things didn't go her way, which was why she made the perfect assistant. She kept things in control the way Julia liked. Control was good. Control kept your business cranking and your life in order without any pesky surprises hiding around any corners.

"You haven't been to The Cage in years. People there miss you."

Wow, Kate was really laying it on thick. The Cage had been another lifetime ago, and one she could barely remember since starting the ad agency.

"What about the McLaughlin account? Did we finish up with that?" Julia asked. "There were a few things I wasn't happy with, and I told James about it. Do you know if he fixed it?"

"Yup. McLaughlin is done. James kicked ass." Kate clicked her pen over and over, a habit that Julia hated. She knew this was just a ploy to get Julia frustrated enough to agree with her. Anything to stop the infernal clicking.

Julia wasn't going to bite. She would wear Kate down first. She casually flipped through her day planner.

"And the Anderson copy? Did that get fixed and

typeset? Because you know how picky they are. We can't afford to lose that account because of one stupid error."

Kate tapped her foot. "All fixed and perfect."

"Oh, and the Sinclair account. I'm still trying to negotiate…"

"Yes, yes, yes, Julia. James already finished it. Even though you think the poor guy can't do anything. Why did you even take him on if you're afraid to give him work?"

Click. Click. Click.

"I never said James couldn't do anything. It's just that I haven't had a chance to spend as much time with him as I should. I need to see more from him."

"Please stop ignoring the fact that I'm trying to get you out of your stupid house to see some music. You used to go out all the time. You *love* music. Give yourself a break and just have some fun for a change. The business isn't going to shut down if you don't stay late one night. Besides, James can handle it. He rocks."

She had no decent excuse for why she shouldn't go out. Kate was right. For three years she had lived and breathed The Julia Powers Agency, putting other important parts of her life on the backburner. Boyfriends. Friends. Family. *Fun.*

James had taken some of the weight off her back, yet she still had a hard time letting him take over certain aspects of her job, even though she really needed the help. The agency was her baby. While all her friends were off getting married and having kids, she was building a business all by herself. Now she had a multi-million dollar agency and no money worries. People told her she'd never be a success in the crowded field of advertising. But she had proven them wrong. Life was a competition and she was in it to win.

But success came with a price. Keeping track of every detail of a business was exhausting. She was wound tight enough to snap. Maybe going out was what she needed. She might even meet a guy, although that would come with another set of issues. Men didn't understand her. Never had. Her last boyfriend told her she'd rather sleep with her business than sleep with him.

Sadly, he was right.

"Sting, you say?" she asked, peering up at Kate.

Kate rolled her eyes. "Would I lie to you about Sting?"

People knew not to joke with Julia where Sting was concerned. Now *there* was a man who couldn't possibly disappoint her. She'd been in love with him since the first time she heard that voice of his pour through her speakers. Kate must be telling the truth. Maybe she'd let her assistant win this round.

"Okay," Julia sighed. "I'll go."

Kate clapped her hands together. "I can't wait to dress you."

"So my clothes aren't right, either?"

"No, your clothes are totally rad. I just don't think an Armani suit is going to go over very well at The Cave, do you? I've got a pair of green Doc Martens to die for. Your feet are screaming to wear them, don't even deny it. And let's take your hair out of that uptight twist and crimp the hell out of it."

"You got your way. Now shoo." Julia waved her

off with a smile, trying to hold in her laughter as Kate skipped out of her office, her blonde curls bouncing as she hummed a Smith's song.

"Be at your house at nine to turn you into a punk sex kitten!" she called out before shutting Julia's door.

Julia groaned. This was going to be a long night. She was usually in bed by nine. But much to her surprise, she couldn't wait to go.

⚡ TWO

Julia

That familiar club smell hit her the moment she walked through the door. Stale beer, smoke and mold. The Cave hadn't changed one bit. Still run down. Still too small and overcrowded. Same peeling paint and scuffed floor.

She loved it.

Bands fought like hell to get a time slot there. Playing The Cave was a rite of passage and half the groups in *Rolling Stone* had passed through this hole in the wall. At one point in Julia's life it had been like a second home, and she hadn't realized how much she missed this place now that she'd been away from it for so many years.

Kate held her hand up to the bartender and motioned for two beers.

"Is that Julia?" he said, reaching over the bar to hug her. "You look gorgeous, honey. Long time, no see!"

"Thanks, Chet. It's good to be back."

"Heard your business is going well. I always knew you'd break out and do something great. Being a cocktail waitress here never suited you."

"I made a hell of a lot in tips, though." Julia remembered all the beers she lugged through the crowds of drunken patrons. Enough to pay for a good chunk of grad school.

"Don't be a stranger," Chet said, pulling the caps off two beer bottles. "We need more eye candy in this dump."

A large man barreled into her from the side, grabbing her around the arms and squeezing her with the strength of a boa constrictor. "Juuulia," he slurred dramatically. "You look mahvelooouuus."

Andrew. Kate's boyfriend. As tall as a redwood, and even taller with his spiked green mohawk.

"Stop it, you brute. You're going to crush her!" yelled Kate, and whooped as Andrew grabbed Kate around the waist, lifting her like she weighed nothing more than a five-pound bag of sugar.

Julia watched them and couldn't help but be envious. They made an adorable couple. Smart. Talented. So very in love.

Julia wanted what they had, but her relationships had been nothing but huge disappointments. Inevitably, she would be let down. Maybe her standards were too high. But was it so wrong to expect one hundred percent from the person you were sleeping with? She didn't think so. Her time was too precious to waste on anything less than that from a lover.

Which was probably why she hadn't had one in four years.

She swigged her beer and tried to focus on the music. She planned on enjoying this night no matter what, but she would have been just as happy at home in her pajamas, a nice glass of red in hand. She had picked up some new records and couldn't wait to listen to them, to let the music and lyrics fill her up and take her away. Music was the one thing that never let her down.

"This band is going to be super popular. Let's move to the front," Kate bellowed in her ear and grabbed her hand, pulling her through the tangle of bodies towards the edge of the stage. Julia leaned against the scuffed wood, people pushing and shoving around her, jockeying for space. She loved this moment of anticipation before the band came on.

The lights went down and the crowd whistled and hooted as the shadow of three men walked out, one reaching for a guitar resting near the microphone at center stage. Julia couldn't see much of his face, but he looked tall and looming as he adjusted his guitar and leaned toward the microphone.

The crowd hushed as a melancholy riff filled the club. It also filled her body, its sweet sound making its way into her ears, down her throat, and into her stomach like warm syrup, ending in a pool at her feet. She closed her eyes and let the riff carry her away.

She opened her eyes when a familiar voice washed

over her, and found herself looking at a tattooed hand. And a face she knew all too well.

Matthew.

🎸 THREE

Matthew

The first strum on the strings zipped through his fin gers like an electric current, lighting him up from head to toe. He lived for this feeling. This buzz. Nothing compared to it. Not drugs nor alcohol. Not even sex. Well, sex might, but he couldn't remember the last time he'd had it. Maybe a year? Fuck, how could that even be possible? He needed to fix that and goddamn soon.

Matthew shook away that depressing thought and switched off, letting the music take over his mind and body until he was nothing more than a vehicle for sound. The band hit their stride by their second song, guitar, drums and bass communicating on a higher level. The front half of the club bounced up and down like pogo sticks and the energy in the club was off the charts.

This could turn out to be a really special night for the band. The manager of the club had mentioned that Seymour Klein, a New York record exec with one of the best labels, would be there tonight. This could finally be the break Joyride had been waiting for. And, man, was he ever ready for that break.

A contract meant making enough money to finally have more time for the band. Maybe he could even take on a few more guitar students when he wasn't on tour. If he had a record deal, he probably wouldn't need the extra cash the lessons brought in, but teaching really wasn't about the money. It was about the look of awe on the face of a student who finally figured out how to play their favorite song. It always reminded him of his own life-changing moment at age eleven when he realized exactly what he wanted to do with his life.

But the day job? *Fuck.* It felt like purgatory. Like tiny slices of his soul being stripped away, one stinking onion layer at a time. Being a manager made it even worse. Most days it was like herding cats. How hard was it to get to work on time and do your job? His work ethic didn't include being late or slacking off. He'd been on his own and working his ass off since he was eighteen, and he needed that record deal like he needed air in his lungs.

He often daydreamed about walking out, mostly during lunchtime when the crush of hungry assholes in their bespoke suits came in and treated him like shit. And how about all the sharp cutlery just waiting to slice off one of his digits? He had narrowly missed his thumb with a chef's knife more than once. He'd rather be dead than not be able to play the guitar anymore. Just dig the hole and chuck him in.

But then that pretty girl started to come in every few days, and suddenly work didn't seem all that bad. He could smell her before he could see her. She smelled like freshly cut flowers and he wanted to run his fingers through her dark brown hair, bury his head into her neck, and just breathe her in.

But it wasn't just her looks that intrigued him. The girl *knew music*. He got to play his boom box at the shop, and spent hours putting together mix tapes that would make the miserable drudge go by faster. He even threw some of Joyride's songs in once in a while, just to see customers' reactions. She was waiting for her sandwich one day when it came on — his song. She stood in his line wearing her expensive suit, her head bobbing back and forth to the rhythm. She even hummed the chorus.

"You like this song?" he asked, shocked that someone who looked like her could like music like his. That was the first sentence he had ever spoken to her.

"It's so catchy." He liked her hoarse voice.

"I like it, too," he said, and went back to making her the best fucking turkey sandwich she would ever have in her entire life.

"Who is it? His voice is great."

"Some new band. Joyride." Matthew leaned over the counter and handed her the paper-wrapped sandwich.

"I'll have to check them out," she said with a smile.

To say that his heart swelled with pride would be an understatement.

The next week she handed him a receipt, black writing scrawled on the back of it. "These are some bands I really like, and well, I thought maybe you'd want to check them out." She seemed shy. Even embarrassed. He stuffed that list in his jeans pocket and guarded it with his life. And wouldn't you know it? He loved every band on that shiny scrap of paper. Each week, he couldn't wait to see what she would bring in for him. Someday, maybe he'd be brave enough to find out her name.

Screw it. If he could stand on stage and lay himself bare, then he could grow a pair and ask a pretty girl for her goddamn name. He was definitely going to take it a step further the next time she came in.

So maybe it was just the high he was getting from playing, or else he had really begun to lose his mind, but the girl in the front row looked an awful lot like her. Only the hair and eye makeup were all wrong. *But that mouth.* He knew that crimson mouth. Had dreamed about kissing it. What the hell was she doing in a shithole like The Cave? And with his friend Andrew?

Sweat poured off Matthew as Joyride jammed through their last song. He wanted to stay swept up in the rhythm forever and just let all the other shit he had to deal with fade away. When their set came to a close, he searched for her under the blue and red lights. He needed to see her one more time. Just to be sure.

But she was gone.

᠁ ᠁ ᠁

Matthew wiped the sweat off his neck with a rough towel and scanned the backstage area. If you could even call it that. It was more of a stinky, small room with black walls and folding chairs, cheap beer and off-label booze. Whoever said the club life was glamorous had apparently never been backstage at The Cave.

He found Andrew in the corner, swigging some crap domestic beer and laughing with their drummer, Coop. No sign of the girl anywhere.

"Andrew, buddy!" Matthew said, putting a hand on his shoulder and clinking beers. "What did you think of the show?"

"Off the hook, man. Off the *hook*!" Andrew said, slapping Matthew on the back. "You make it look so damn easy."

It was easy. As easy as breathing. If only the rest of his life would follow suit. "Listen, there was a girl with you tonight, right in the front. Is she a friend of yours?"

"You mean my girlfriend? Come on, man, give a brother a break. I can't compete with you."

"No, not Kate, you ass. But now that you say it, Kate *is* very pretty..." Matthew raised his brow. "No, seriously. She had long brown hair? Tons of black eyeliner? She looks like someone that comes into the shop all the time."

"Oh, *that girl*. That's Julia. Kate's boss. Her office is right near your work." Andrew wiggled his eyebrows. "And I'm pretty sure she's single. Interested?"

So her office was close to the shop. It had to be her. What were the odds that she'd know Andrew, too? Not that it really mattered. Finally, he had a name. *Julia*. He repeated it silently until it began to take the shape of something that made his pulse quicken. "Nope. Just curious. I thought she looked familiar, that's all."

Andrew slapped Matthew's back again, almost breaking a rib. "You look a little more than curious, big guy. Too bad she needed to leave early. I could have introduced you. You think you're ready to date a big bad boss lady?"

"Who said anything about dating? Jesus, can't a guy ask about a girl without wanting to get her into bed?"

"Nope," Andrew laughed.

Matthew swigged a third beer. Goddamn it all to hell. He hadn't felt any stirrings down below in a long time, not until Julia walked through the door and rocked his world. And it had to be for Kate's boss. *Kate's goddamn boss.* Of all the dumb luck. That made her the owner of the ad agency. A very successful and powerful advertising agency.

Older. Sophisticated. And way out of his league.

He had started to believe that she kinda liked him. But how could a successful woman like her ever be interested in a young punk like him? Was he reading too much into those scraps of paper? He didn't think so. Christ, he was so confused. He needed more booze. He stopped counting the beers and began to fall into a fuzzy cocoon of not giving a damn. By the time his bassist, John, dropped him off at his apartment, he had forgotten all about a woman called Julia. Hell, he'd practically forgotten his own name.

Until he woke up the next morning and it all came

flooding back like an anvil to his skull. And he was out of aspirin.

Julia.

Fuck.

🎸 FOUR

Julia

Julia was going to punch Andrew the next time she saw him. She knew he'd given Kate the idea to buy her guitar lessons for her birthday. She should never have mentioned to them that night at the Joyride show that she always regretted not learning how to play. Apparently, this teacher was Andrew's friend. "The best freakin' guitar teacher ever," was how he had put it.

Thirty-five and just learning a musical instrument. She couldn't be sure if this was one of those "you're still young and can learn so many things" moments, or a "we feel so bad you're old… better learn something before you die" moments. Maybe she had looked extra pathetic at the club the other night, drooling over Matthew as his forearms flexed and his brow sweat, and they figured she needed an outlet for all her pent-up sexual energy. Beating the shit out of a guitar could be just what she needed. Or maybe this was all part of their plan to get Julia out of her condo to have some fun for a change, before she withered into an old spinster.

She threw her father's beat up acoustic guitar case over her shoulder, and set out for a walk to MG Music at number eight 1114 Liberty Road. The skies opened up halfway there and soaked her through, her Police concert T-shirt clinging to her like a second skin, hair dripping down her back. Her feet made squishing sounds in her red Converse. Mother Nature was a first class bitch.

She reached the address and dashed into the vestibule filled with copies of free newspapers and unwanted mail, but hesitated before ringing any bell. This didn't look like a school or a business. She had assumed she would be taking lessons at a reputable, public place, not an apartment building. Did she really want to go into some guy's apartment she didn't know? Andrew said this person was a great teacher. As difficult as it was to ignore her gut feeling that this was a bad idea, she had to trust Andrew. Why would a friend steer her wrong?

None of the doorbells were labeled MG Music, but there was one that said M. Gordon, number eight. Frustrated, she pressed it, and waited. And waited. How long was she actually supposed to stand here? She was giving this M. Gordon just one more minute of her time and then she was gone.

Just as she was ready to leave, she heard a loud buzz, and pushed open the heavy wooden door.

"I'm on the third floor," came a deep voice from the stairwell above. "Come on up, door's open."

With each step she climbed, she attempted to make herself look half decent, but it was a losing battle. To make matters worse, her nipples were standing at full attention in her wet T-shirt. She tried draping her long, soaking hair over the front of Sting, Stewart and Andy's faces to cover them up. Mascara was probably dripping down her face, but she didn't have a mirror to fix it. Her business--hell, her entire life--was all about carefully controlled first impressions, and now she was ashamed that she was going to be making a really bad one.

She reached the third floor and saw that the apartment to the left had its door open. Was she supposed to just walk right in? Why wasn't M. Gordon at the door, greeting her like a normal person? No manners. Another strike. Maybe she should turn and go, gift be damned. She could tell Andrew and Kate to give the lessons to someone else, that she needed her Saturdays to do more important things than goofing around with childish guitars and impolite people who didn't know how to say hello properly.

"Here, I figured you'd need this." He came out of the apartment and walked toward her with a towel, and when they looked at each other, everything stopped. His steps. Her breathing. Even her hair stopped dripping.

"Roasted turkey on whole wheat with cranberry? What are you doing here?"

MG Music.

M. Gordon.

Matthew Gordon.

Matthew.

But she couldn't say his name. In fact, she couldn't do much of anything at all except stare at him and drop her guitar case with a heavy thud that echoed through the stairwell.

"Take this," he said, offering her the towel. "You're soaking."

Then he walked back into his apartment. Was she supposed to follow him? Or just stand there? Why didn't she know what to do with herself? Why wasn't he asking her in?

"You can come in, you know," he called out.

She wrapped the towel around her chest, grabbed the guitar case, and went in.

His apartment smelled like laundry just out of the dryer. Julia loved that smell. It reminded her of when she was a kid in the wintertime, wearing freshly washed, warm flannel pajamas, and tucked safely in bed. She had felt totally taken care of, not worrying about a thing except what Barbie doll to play with, and whether or not her mom was making cookies or brownies for after-school. She longed for that carefree kid feeling again. Life seemed so easy, not like now. Adulthood could really suck.

She glanced around his small but spotless kitchen. A stovetop espresso maker sat empty on the nicked and worn Formica counter, above which ran a shelf lined with cookbooks. Photos were scattered on his fridge door, newspapers and books strewn on every available surface. It was the exact opposite of her sterile condo where nothing was ever out of place. Normally, she would feel uncomfortable around all this clutter, but for some reason, it made her feel at ease. Like she could hang out and just *be*. The more she looked around, the more she thought the whole place suited him. He always seemed so easygoing at work, even when they were slammed. His apartment had that same relaxed vibe.

He came out of his bedroom holding a sweatshirt. "You can wear this. I just washed it. Promise."

"Thank you." She took it from him.

"Ah, she speaks!"

Julia laughed. "Sorry. This is just…"

"Weird?" he said while she put on his sweatshirt emblazoned with a Buckley College of Music logo. It came down to her knees.

"Yes, that." She felt better now that she was covered up and had some control of her vocal chords again. She used the towel to squeeze out her hair and wipe under her eyes, hoping she didn't look as awful as she thought. "I had no idea you were going to be my teacher."

Matthew leaned casually against his kitchen table and watched her with a half grin on his face. He wore a T-shirt and she could now see the full-sleeve tattoo on his left arm. Brilliantly colored koi fish swirled around his forearm, biceps and triceps.

Matthew pointed to his arm. "They're a symbol for creativity and aspiration. In case you were wondering."

"I've only seen the corner of it, you know, at lunch." She looked away, embarrassed that she had been caught staring.

"When Andrew said there would be a Jules coming

to take lessons, I assumed it was a guy. I see now that Jules is absolutely *not* a guy."

She extended her hand. "Andrew calls me Jules. But I go by Julia. And I have no idea why I never told you before."

"Matthew. But you already know that. You know, the stupid nametag and all." He gripped her hand and she could feel a callus on his thumb. His strumming thumb. He rubbed it lightly against her wrist and warmth spread up her arm. Well, not exactly warmth. More like flames licking up her arm and zapping all her girlie parts. "And I don't know why I never asked."

He had a small pockmark on his forehead and a faint silvery scar under his right eye. She wanted to ask him how he got it. She wanted to rub her finger along the raised skin and then kiss it.

She pulled her hand away before self-immolation occurred and she melted into his linoleum floor. "And how do you know Andrew?"

"We went to Buckley together for a little while." He pointed at the sweatshirt.

"That's such a coincidence because his girlfriend Kate just happens to be my assistant."

He nodded. "Ah, yes, I saw you two together. At the show."

"You saw me there?"

"Well, you were in the front row. Sorta hard to miss." Matthew rubbed at his stubbly jaw. "Did you enjoy the show?"

"It was amazing. And so weird to be back. I used to waitress there a long time ago."

"Really? That's wild. Anyway, here I am being rude. Would you like something to drink?"

"I'm good," Julia said, hugging herself in his soft sweatshirt, knowing that when the time came, she wouldn't want to give it back to him.

"Well, I was just about to make coffee and you're more than welcome to have some. And then I guess we can talk about the lessons? That's if you still want to do them. I'd understand if you didn't."

Did she? It was going to be awkward being alone with the guy she'd been fantasizing about. But something about the simple act of him standing in front of her, offering to make her coffee, made her want to stay. "No, I do want to. Do you still want to teach me?"

"I'm game if you are, Miss Roasted Turkey on Whole Wheat," he said, and walked over to the stove to grab the espresso pot.

Matthew didn't really walk. He sauntered like he knew his place in the world and didn't mind taking up all the space he could get. He had a star quality, even behind the counter in a mundane place like the sandwich shop. And it came through even stronger on stage. It made you want to touch him. Know him. Rub against him like a cat. Or climb him like a tree.

"Should I sit?" she asked, still unsure of what was supposed to happen next. She finally recognized this unfamiliar emotion, and she hadn't felt it in ages: awkwardness. She didn't like it. She was used to controlling every social situation in her life. Now, she had no idea what to do.

"Have a seat in the living room. There are some music books on the coffee table. You can flip through them and see if there's a song that catches your eye."

She didn't need to look through a book to find that. What caught her eye stood a few feet away from her, grinding espresso beans and measuring water with the concentration of a scientist. For Christ's sake, he made actual *real espresso*. The last guy she'd been with used toilet paper as a coffee filter, rather than get his lazy ass to the supermarket. And he had expected her to drink it.

Animal.

She took a seat on his worn leather couch and thumbed through one of the music books, but the pages blurred into one big scary musical note, so she shut it and checked out some of his albums instead. His taste ran all over the place. A hefty dose of jazz and classical. Classic rock. Punk. New Wave. She owned many of the same LPs and cassettes.

"So what made you decide to take guitar lessons?" he called from the kitchen.

"I didn't really. Well, I did. I do. My dad plays and I always wanted to learn, but just never found the time. This was a surprise birthday gift from Andrew and Kate."

"Well, it's really turned out to be quite the surprise, right?" He joined her in the living room holding two small espresso cups. "Now, may I present you with the best coffee ever."

"Ever? We'll see about that. I've had the best coffee ever, and it's across the ocean in a tiny café in Italy." She realized how pretentious that sounded as soon as it came out of her mouth. She wished her mouth would just shut up.

Matthew smirked. "I think I'd hold off on any decision until you've actually tasted it."

There were two other places to sit in the room, but Matthew chose the spot right next to her on the couch.

"How long have you been teaching?" She took a sip of his coffee. Goddamn. He was right. It was freakin' delicious.

"Wow, let's see. A few years. I kinda fell into it. I started doing it for the money, but now I love it so much I'd probably do it for free. I mean, The Sandwich Factory pays management pretty well, but that's certainly not my life's dream, you know? Joyride is my main focus. I want us to go national."

"I had no idea your band was the one you've been playing at lunch. You guys are really great. Why didn't you tell me?"

"Keep your fingers crossed, but we could be looking at a major record deal soon. And if that happens, man, I am out of here so fast."

Julia played with the wet, frayed cuffs of her jeans. The thought of him leaving made her unexpectedly sad. "So that's your dream then, to be a rock star?"

"I just want to make money doing what I love. And that's playing music. Always has been. The rock star stuff would just be the ultimate icing. So what about you? You're in advertising, right?"

"Yup, I own an agency."

"Mighty impressive for someone so young."

"Well, I've always known I wanted to be my own

boss. I have a teensy little problem with people telling me what to do. That's why I didn't last too long as a waitress."

She figured she'd leave out the fact that most people called her the yard boss when she was a kid, and also how she wouldn't consider herself *young* exactly. She still hadn't tackled her mixed feelings regarding their age difference. If she calculated correctly, he was probably in his mid-twenties. She had never dated anyone younger before. Sure, the idea was taboo and thrilling, but she worried what other people would think of her dating someone who was pooping his diaper while she was meandering the halls of junior high school, plastering her walls with pop stars, and wondering when her boobs were finally going to grow.

But she was getting ahead of herself. Because they weren't dating. They were just two people sharing a cup of coffee. A teacher and his student. The fact that she wanted to kiss him made no difference, because let's face it, the chances were slim that he had any desire to *kiss her*. She was way too old for him.

"That's very good to know about you, Julia, seeing that I'm going to be telling you what to do. A lot," he laughed. "I hope I won't have to put you in time out for *misbehaving*."

He really needed to stop making innuendo like that or else she was going to slide right off the couch. They didn't have the buffer of the sandwich counter between them anymore. At least there, she knew nothing could happen. Flirting could be innocent. It's not like he was going to hop over the glass counter and take her right there on the tile floor, although goodness knows she had thought about it happening more than once. But here in his apartment, the possibilities were endless. She needed to stop thinking about those possibilities.

But, Christ, he was sexy as hell. Sexier than any man she had ever met, young or old.

He grabbed her guitar case and removed her father's Martin. "This is *sweet*."

"It's pretty beat up and old," she said. "My dad used to play songs for me when I was little, so it's pretty special to me."

Matthew fiddled with the tuners as he strummed. "Nice mellow sound. And real easy to learn on." He handed it to her and she tried to position it on her lap. "You look good with a guitar, Jules."

She found the comment ironic, because to be honest, she felt very awkward holding it, and she had a sudden, terrifying feeling that this guitar lesson thing wasn't going to be as easy as she had thought.

What if she couldn't do this?

He didn't seem to notice that she was frozen in fear as he kept on talking. "By the way, thanks again for all those recommendations you gave me. Some pretty great stuff on those lists. I especially loved that Joy Division tune. Wasn't really into them before, but those bass lines are killer."

"Right?" she said, picking at the strings and trying to get the instrument to feel comfortable. It wasn't working. She had played with the guitar for fun when she was a kid, back when she could barely get her arms around it. Now it felt like someone had stuck a tree trunk on her lap and expected her to make it do something.

He finished his coffee and scooted forward on the couch, his hands resting on his knees. "So I usually start every lesson by asking one very important question."

God, what was he going to ask her? She felt her back tense up. She just knew she was going to get it wrong, whatever it was. She had been totally unprepared for anything that had happened to her today, and her nerves were about to unravel.

Still, she nodded, as if she could ace any question in the world.

"Tell me. What do you love about music?"

🎸 FIVE

Matthew

H oly shit.
 Julia.

He could not stop thinking about her. The shock of seeing her standing in his hallway, dripping wet, T-shirt clinging to those perfect breasts. Sitting on his couch. Wearing his goddamn clothes. Drinking out of his cups. Touching his albums. The sweet smell of her had lingered long after she left, driving him crazy.

He had tried hard to keep it together that first lesson. To appear nonchalant and all teacher-like, while his insides did cartwheels. She was even more beautiful up close. He could see the freckles that dusted the bridge of her nose and the thin rings of gold around the deep brown of her eyes. He could fall into those eyes and just hang out for a good long while.

He paced his apartment, waiting for the buzz that meant she decided to come to her next lesson. She hadn't been in for lunch all week, and he feared that she wouldn't be showing up today because, to be perfectly honest, their first lesson hadn't gone well at all. She hadn't been lying when she said she didn't like people telling her what to do. He'd picked up on the frustration in her eyes while he was showing her the chords and she wasn't getting it. She tried to come up with some good excuses, like her nails were too long. Or she was tired and having a hard time focusing. But he knew better. Had seen it so many times before. Just because you loved music didn't mean you'd be able to play it. In fact, he wouldn't be surprised if she quit, which would be a real shame because he hated when any student wanted to give up. It meant he wasn't doing his job. And if she quit, it would also mean he wouldn't get the chance to be alone with her anymore.

And he absolutely wanted to be alone with her.

Everything about her turned him on, even her hands. He'd pressed his fingers against hers as they held down chords together and Matthew memorized every little detail about them. How small they were compared to his. How pale and unmarred, unlike his callused and scarred up ones. How would they feel on his face? His chest? Or anything due south of his belly button? His pants had tightened just thinking about it, and he felt like a teenager daydreaming about the prettiest girl in class and having to hide his crotch with a history book.

Not cool. Luckily he'd had a guitar in front of him to disguise the embarrassing evidence.

Her answer to his question about music had especially floored and excited him. She talked about the mythology and nostalgia of songs. How music was like a never-ending soundtrack to her life. How she felt it in the marrow of her bones. He felt the same way, but had yet to find anyone to put those feelings into words the way she had.

But man, he was going to have his job cut out for him. He prided himself on being a patient teacher, and knew he could probably get her sounding halfway decent, but she was going to have to work really hard at it. Some students just picked it up right away, as if playing guitar was second nature. Not Julia, and it didn't take much for him to figure out that her competitive nature was going to be her downfall.

Ten more minutes went by. He had almost convinced himself that it would be for the best if she didn't show up, and they could go back to their respective roles as sandwich maker and sandwich eater. Besides, he didn't need anything complicating his life, not with a potential record deal on the horizon. Did he really need a smoking hot older woman to distract him? One who felt the same way about music as he did? Who carried her first ever concert ticket in her wallet, and told him her favorite band was Zeppelin?

Yes, he absolutely fucking did.

He was so screwed.

Julia Powers. Miss Turkey on Whole Wheat, with her smile that lit up the room. He had started looking forward to those weekly song lists like water in the desert. The disappointment of not seeing her this past week felt palpable.

Buzz. Buzz. Buzz.

He raced to his door and pressed that goddamn buzzer faster than light.

"I'm late. I'm so sorry," she called to him as she made her way up the stairs. Gone were the ripped jeans and T-shirt. She wore a tight red dress, her dark hair piled up into a twist, stray pieces framing her flushed cheeks.

"I really hate being late. I've been away all week. Unexpected business. A real ball buster of a client, but I totally won him over. I just landed, but if you don't have time for me, I understand. I just didn't want to leave you hanging and I didn't have your number with me."

He wanted to dance across the room. He wanted to write lyrics for her. He was fucking gone. "Take a breath, Whole Wheat, it's okay. You made it. I still have some time."

Who was he kidding? He had all the time in the world. Band practice could wait.

She sat at his old kitchen table and sighed heavily. Her under eyes looked faintly bruised, her skin pale, giving her an ethereal appearance. He wanted to tell her that she looked like an angel at his table. One with a little bit of devil mixed in. Christ, *that dress*. And there went the tightening in his pants again.

"Have you eaten? Do you want a grilled cheese?" he asked, quickly turning his back to begin gathering the ingredients out of the fridge. She looked like she needed to eat. He desperately needed to hide his hard on.

She perked up. "Did you just read my mind? I love grilled cheese. But only on white bread. And seriously, only if you have time."

"White bread is the only respectable way it should be eaten. You're talking to the master of grilled cheese over here."

She wagged her finger at him. "I'm pretty sure there's no way yours is going to be better than mine. *I'm* a master at grilled cheese."

He pulled a spatula off the rack and smacked his thigh with it. "Did you just make this a competition, Jules? Because I'm sorry to say you're totally going to lose. Badly. Remember the coffee incident?"

"That was just a fluke," she said, a gleam in her eye. "Luck."

Matthew got to work buttering the bread, chuckling to himself.

He put the sandwiches on the griddle and watched her as she placed one of his cheap white napkins on her lap and fiddled with his hand-me-down placemats. What did she think about him? About the way he lived? She looked like a priceless piece of art, out of place at his worn kitchen table, and he suddenly felt ashamed of his apartment. His menial job. He could only imagine what her house looked like – all modern furniture and prints from fancy galleries. Certainly nothing like his one-bedroom filled with old furniture and used paperbacks. But if he had that contract, things would change. He would be on her level. Worthy of a woman like her. Problem was, he hadn't heard a word from Klein yet and it was starting to upset him. Matthew knew his band rocked. Now the rest of the world needed to know it, too.

He plated the grilled cheese, handed it to her on an old, chipped China plate, and sat across from her. "Go ahead, Whole Wheat. Take a bite."

She took a dainty bite, careful not to smear her lipstick. Her eyes widened. She took another, a bigger one this time. She closed her eyes and hummed. She actually *hummed* while chewing. Could there be anything sexier than a gorgeous woman in a tight red dress humming while she ate your food?

Absolutely fucking not.

"So I'm guessing it's totally rad?" he asked.

She waited a moment too long to answer him, just long enough to kinda piss him off.

"I wouldn't go that far."

"Your actions speak louder than your noisy mouth full of cheese."

"Hmm, well, the bread to cheese ratio is somewhat lacking. I would have used three pieces rather than two. The bread could be a tad crispier. Otherwise, I'd have to say this narrowly ranks in my top ten."

He held on to the edge of the table and leaned back on two chair legs. "Do you mind if I ask you a question? What's this obsession you have with winning?" He immediately regretted having asked the question. It could offend her, but he needed to figure out how she ticked if they were ever going to make this whole lesson thing work. Or anything else. And he really, really wanted some *anything else* with her.

She wiped her mouth with his thin napkin and

raised an eyebrow. "What, are you asking me if I know I'm competitive?"

"I guess. Yes, that's what I'm asking."

She balled up the napkin and tossed it on the table. "I've been told. I just want to be the best at anything I do. Otherwise, what's the point?"

"The point? What about just having fun? Who even cares if you're not the best? All the great stuff happens in the trying, in my opinion, at least."

"Well, I guess we have different opinions."

Damn, she was infuriating. Could he even deal with infuriating? He seriously wondered if there was any way he could succeed in teaching her. Not when she couldn't even see that her desire to be right was going to cancel out any chance of her truly enjoying the learning process. He'd taught too many students for too many years not to know what was coming. She was going to set the bar too high, and even though she would never be a failure in his eyes, she would be a failure in her own, and that was something he couldn't teach her to get over.

But still, there was something about her that got under his skin —had been since the moment she stood in his line, hands on her hips, and told him how she wanted her lunch made in precise goddamn detail, like he'd never made a fucking turkey sandwich before. He wanted to kiss her senseless and tell her to piss off, all at the same time.

Then she handed him that list. The list that had him running to the record store and hunting down everything on it. How many nights did he sit alone in Joyride's practice space, turntable blasting out some amazing song that made him smile his ass off because he knew she loved it, too? How many gatefolds did he study, blown away by the fact that it came out when he was just a kid? How many new songs did he write with her on his mind?

Whether she realized it or not, Julia was giving him way more than just music with those lists. That beautiful control freak was offering up little slips of her heart.

And goddamn if he was going to give up on someone like that.

🎸 SIX

Julia

Fuck Matthew and his perfect grilled cheese. And coffee.

Fuck Matthew and his precise, beautifully messed up hands that made guitar strings bend and sing at his whim.

Everything he touched became magic. Even food. If the way he handled his instrument was any indication, his hands would probably feel like angel wings fluttering against her skin. Matthew made everything appear effortless, as if the world worked to accommodate him, and not the other way around. What would it feel like to go through life that way? She fought and scraped through her life. If she let her guard down for one second, someone else might come along and take it all away from her. Her desire to win, to be the best, was all-consuming. She rarely failed at anything.

But she had a feeling she would be failing guitar lessons. How fucking embarrassing was that?

Her first lesson had been deplorable. The stupid guitar felt awkward and heavy in her arms. The strings too hard to hold. The frets merged into a bunch of white dots that mocked her. She couldn't get her hands to do two different things at the same time. It was as if they belonged to someone else. Someone with no coordination or rhythm.

She outright sucked.

And in front of Matthew, of all people.

So why hadn't she just skipped the lesson and driven home, rather than head straight to Matthew's from the airport for more humiliation?

Because the idea of not seeing him hurt more than making a fool of herself in front of him. At least it did until he suggested they try again. Well, what had she expected him to do? Just sit there and chat with her?

Kiss her?

"Let's try to get some of your lesson in before I need to leave for band practice. Don't want to cheat you out of your time."

She could now see that coming here had been a mistake, but her hormones had wiped out any logical thinking. She really didn't want to play. In fact, she wanted to quit, but didn't know how to tell him.

"I didn't bring my guitar. Honest, don't worry about the lesson. I know I came really late, and you should leave for practice. Practice is more important."

Matthew put his hand on her shoulder. "I don't want you to leave. You came all this way. Go grab one of mine and let's at least review what we did last week."

Dread gripped her as she chose the oldest-looking acoustic of the bunch. No sense ruining one of his nicer guitars with her pathetic and painful playing. Her palms were already sweating. There was no way she was getting out of this. And it was no one's fault but her own.

"Ah, my favorite guitar," he said, settling down on the couch and opening up the music book. "And also my first."

"Don't tell me I picked out the one you lost your virginity to. Maybe I should put her back? She might get jealous."

Truth be told, *she* was the jealous one. That lucky guitar got to feel Matthew's hands on it, and only Matthew's, for its entire life.

"I was eleven when she deflowered me. I think she'll survive. I've been stepping out on her for many years now. But back to the lesson. Last week we touched upon C, A, G, E and D, or CAGED, like I told you. Why don't you try C for a bit and then we can move on from there."

Julia sat on the edge of the couch, hands shaking. She couldn't remember anything about C except the feel of his hands on hers last week when he tried to show her where it was. That she remembered all too well. Well enough to keep her up at night, antsy and frustrated for his touch.

"Sure. So C is right... here..." She positioned her fingers on the frets, hoping she was at least close enough to C so she didn't look like a total idiot. She hadn't practiced. Hadn't even looked at her guitar since last week.

She strummed a few times. The guitar sounded out of tune and tinny. Matthew watched her with a smirk on his face and she wanted to shrink into the couch cushions.

"Someone didn't practice this week, did they," he said. "I think you just invented your own chord."

"I was busy all week," she shot back. Christ, she sounded harsh. Why couldn't she just admit that she was too afraid to practice?

"Hey, don't get upset. You could have just told me. Let me show you again. Just try to remember this placement for C." He rested his fingers on hers. "Now get a firm grip on the strings and don't let go. Just practice strumming and get used to the way this feels. Just like you did before."

The way he said *grip* gave her chills, like he was talking about her gripping something other than the guitar neck. She wanted him to keep saying things like *firm* and *strum*. She wanted him to put his lips on her shoulder. The nape of her neck. Maybe run his hands through her hair.

"Nope, you keep slipping. Hold them tighter. You'll eventually need to learn how to slide up and down without letting up on the firmness."

Holy God.

She tried to ignore her dirty thoughts and concentrate. Seriously, how hard could it be to strum on some strings and make it sound pleasant? She ran a million-dollar company. She could close a deal better than anyone. But this guitar thing? Brutal.

"I think I see part of your problem. Put Gracie down for a minute."

"Gracie? It has a *name*?"

He shook out his arms and scrunched his shoulders. "Do what I do. Loosen up. And yes, I named *her*. There's Gracie, Sadie, Sandy, Ruby and Betty." He pointed to the four other guitars resting on stands in the living room corner.

"Is that some kind of weird musician thing?"

"Just do what I do," he said again, craning his neck from side to side and flexing his fingers with a crack. When he raised his arms above his head, his Beat concert T-shirt rode up, and she could see the band of his striped boxers and that delicious line of sin that started just below his belly button. What other tattoos might he be hiding? Would she ever get to discover them?

"If I'd known we were doing Jane Fonda's aerobics class, I would have worn my leg warmers." She felt out of breath, but not from the exercise. Matthew was now bent over, his ass up in the air. And, oh, what a fine ass it was. Levi's had never looked so good.

He straightened out to his full height. "Is that you asking to borrow my clothes again?"

"No. Besides, you're a giant. That sweatshirt fits me like a mini-dress. What are you, like, seven feet tall?"

"I'm six three. And you better bring that back at some point. It's my favorite. Now, please, focus. You want to be as loose as possible. We hold a lot of tension and stress in our upper body. And that makes playing the guitar difficult. And I can tell your upper body is like cement."

She stopped stretching and furrowed her brow at him. "What's that supposed to mean? That I look hunched over or something?" Did she look like crooked old witch with a hump on her back?

"No, did I say that? Whole Wheat, don't be so sensitive. All I'm getting at is that you work in an office, so you sit most of the time. You probably use a typewriter and that makes your whole neck area stiff. In order to become one with the guitar, your body needs to flow right into it. It becomes an extension of yourself. And eventually, with a lot of practice, it becomes effortless. We can also work on breathing, but we don't have time for that today."

After a few more minutes of twisting and turning, her neck making unnatural cracking sounds, they returned to the lesson.

He settled back into the couch and took an exaggerated deep breath. "See, don't you feel better? More relaxed? The band does this before every show. I'm telling you, it works."

She would never feel relaxed sitting so close to him, or even in the same room with him. Excited? Yes. Awkward? Definitely. But relaxed? Absolutely not.

"Let's give it another try. And remember, the guitar is a part of your body. It will do what you want it to do if you treat it the right way. There's no need to beat it into submission. Deal?"

She raised her eyebrow at his comment, but Gracie

did feel a bit better in her arms now. She concentrated on relaxing her shoulders and letting her neck fall forward. Then she took a deep breath, tentatively put her left fingers on C, and strummed. A sound came out that didn't resemble a dying whale. In fact, it sounded almost pleasant.

"Sounding better," Matthew encouraged. "Just keep concentrating."

She tried a few more times, focusing on finger placement, but then she slipped. And she couldn't remember where fucking C was again, and when she tried one more time, the sound that emanated made Matthew flinch, the small bit of confidence she had gained crumbling inside of her.

"Told you we needed to work on this more," he said. "Slow and steady wins the race."

The next round was even worse, her sore fingertips betraying her. How could she be so freaking bad at this *one thing*?

She put the guitar down with a huff. "I think I'm all set for today."

"Jules, come on, you just started. You can't pitch a fit because you don't get it on the first try. Man, you're harder to teach than my eight-year-olds."

She threw him a look that could kill. "What's that supposed to mean?"

"They're a lot easier on themselves, that's what it means."

"Yeah, well, thanks for that," she said, crossing her arms.

Matthew had the nerve to laugh at her. She hated

when people laughed at her. How could he find any of this funny?

"Come on. Lighten up. It's just guitar. There's no award for being the best. Oh, wait, don't tell me. Were you, like, valedictorian or something? That would explain so much."

"As a matter of fact, Matthew, I was. And summa cum laude at university. For undergrad *and* grad."

He clapped his hands. "I was right. Of *course* you were."

"Being the best is important to me. Don't laugh."

"Just tell me one thing. Do you ever have any fun? You know, let that hair down? Try and fail at something and not get upset about it because you had a blast just trying?"

Matthew moved toward her, closing the space between them. She wanted to push him away for being so annoying, but her arms wouldn't work. "Of course I have," she said, her heart racing the closer he got. He put his warm hands on her shoulders and her knees became wobbly.

Her face barely reached his mid-chest, and if she leaned her head slightly forward, she could rest her head on his pecs. Did he have a hairy chest? Or smooth? She bet he had a six-pack. And what about that glorious hip dip?

"I know how to have fun, Matthew, if that's what you're getting at."

But she wasn't so sure about that anymore. She hated to admit it, but what Matthew was saying hit way too close to home. She had never followed through on anything she didn't nail on her first try. The fact that he had already figured this out about her, after such a short time, was unnerving. He knew how to get under her skin and press all her tender, vulnerable spots. And she hated it.

"Playing music is all about fun. And passion. That's why I have this heart on my hand. To remind myself every time I play that I'm doing what I love. Even on the bad nights. But it doesn't seem that way for you. Am I wrong?"

She avoided his gaze. "Failing is weakness."

His hands found the back of her neck and he let his fingers play along her skin, the best kind of chills traveling down her spine. "What are you failing at? Playing C?"

Hearing him say it made her feel stupid. True, it was only a guitar chord. But, oh, it was so much more than that in her mind.

"No one can play on their first few lessons. That's why you need lots and lots of practice. Jesus Christ, give yourself a break. I'm serious."

"In my business, you don't get breaks. It's either pass or fail. I don't know how to be any other way."

"But this isn't your business. This is just *music*. Something you love. No one is judging you here. There is no grade."

His hands had migrated and were now cupping her chin, moving her toward him.

"But you don't understand what I'm …" she whispered, unable to finish her sentence before Matthew placed a finger on her lips.

"Whole Wheat? This is your teacher telling you to stop talking or you're going to be put in time out."

Soft, warm lips brushed against hers. Once. Twice. Then the slightest lick of his tongue against the seam of her mouth.

Of course, Julia had a list of reasons why it would be the *worst* thing in the world to kiss Matthew. Had even written them out, trying to convince herself it would never work out between them. He was too young. She was too old. He was too free and easy. She was too rigid and set in her ways.

But when he licked her lips again, she couldn't help but open up for him. Oh, the heat between them. The softness. The *sweetness*. She could drown in it. His body molded to hers, his knee nudging between her legs so he could get even closer.

Matthew kissed her like he played the guitar - learning her, playing her with such skill. Such tenderness. Making her sing inside. He nipped lightly at her bottom lip, a nearly inaudible sigh escaping her throat. How had she gone her entire life without being kissed like this?

His tongue darted in and out, teasing her. Taunting her. She felt desperate for all of him, bunching up his T-shirt with her hands, and sliding them against the soft skin at his waist. But he didn't move to touch her body. He simply kissed with her with the skill and concentration of someone who studied lip locking for a living. Just when she thought he would go in for the full, passionate kiss she craved, he would take his lips away from hers and tease her with small pecks along her closed eyes, cheeks, and the length of her straining neck. Julia clutched his massive shoulders, his back, his waist, anywhere she could get her hands on him, pulling him tight against her. They fell back clumsily onto the couch and her body melted into the worn leather under the delicious weight of him.

His long body enveloped hers like a blanket, his hands roaming up and down her sides, his fingers finally hooking under the hem of her dress and lifting it up slowly while he caressed her thighs.

"Jules," he whispered in her ear, "Tell me you're okay with this."

Okay with what, exactly? That one question could cover a lot of ground. Okay with having sex? With being a one-night stand? With being the student sleeping with her teacher?

When she didn't answer, he lowered his head, his blonde hair mussed and tickling her skin, and kissed his way down the column of her neck, pushing aside the straps of her dress. He slowly peeled it down, revealing her red lace bra, the one she had worn today secretly hoping he'd get a chance to see it, but knowing he probably wouldn't.

Yet here he was, licking her through the fine French lace. "Perfect," he murmured, tucking his fingers under the fabric and pulling it to the side, revealing her naked breast. He licked her there, flicking his tongue. A soft moan escaped her throat as her body bent at his will. She wanted nothing more than to be touched all over. She wanted his tongue there, and his lips here, and his legs wrapped around everywhere.

His strong hands grasped the small of her back,

bringing their hips together. She could feel his excitement. "So perfect," he whispered into her ear again.

But she wasn't perfect. Far from it. If he stripped away her tough exterior, he'd find a frightened woman. And, wow, was he stripping it. In the form of him dragging her dress down to her waist.

She wanted him. She had no doubt. But she didn't do one-night stands. She didn't give her heart away this easily, to anyone. And she barely knew Matthew. How did young people even do things like this anymore? It had been so long for her. Would she give herself to him, only to find out tomorrow he'd want it from someone else? Some hot groupie that could follow him around on tour and share him with other women? Julia could not share. And she refused to be just some older woman he banged on his couch one Saturday afternoon.

She needed to stop this now before she was too far gone to get herself back. She broke away from their kiss, putting her bra straps in place and pulling up her dress.

"What's wrong?" he asked in a hoarse whisper, looking up at her, his cheeks flushed with desire. "Did I hurt you?"

No, but you will.

"I think we should stop."

She scooted from underneath the tent of his body and he leaned against the back of the couch, his breathing heavy. "Whole Wheat, you're killing me. Stopping is the absolute last thing we should be doing right now."

Julia picked at her kiss-swollen bottom lip, stalling for the right words. Of course, there *were* no right words.

Just a bunch of fucked-up feelings that were making her heart hurt.

"If you don't hurry up and say something, I'm going to think the worst over here." He furrowed his brow. "You gotta talk to me."

"You do know how old I am, right?" she finally asked.

He rubbed at his forehead. "I really don't care. It doesn't matter to me."

"Oh, so the fact that I am…" God, she hated to say it out loud, "…*thirty-five*, and you're what, *twenty-one*, doesn't bother you?"

"No. Not one goddamn bit. And I'm twenty-four, by the way."

"So being with a woman my age doesn't weird you out?" she repeated, giving him another chance. To do what, exactly? To stop wanting to kiss and touch her?

He took her face in his hands. "Jules, I'm no fucking kid. I've been on my own since I was eighteen. I think the question you should be asking is does being with *me* bother *you*?"

His last few words felt like taking a bullet. She had wanted him for months. Had fantasized about this very moment. Then why the hell was she pushing him away? Why couldn't she just let go and give this a chance?

He stood up, his erection straining at his jeans. Clearly, he wanted her, but she had ruined it with her need to compartmentalize and analyze the hell out of every emotion and action in her life so nothing bad could ever happen to her.

Not even fun. *Not even love.*

A few more minutes passed, their breathing the only

sound in the room. He was waiting for her answer. She didn't have one.

"Listen, I need to take a shower and get to band practice." He offered his hand and helped her off the couch.

She could have said so many things to him at that moment. Things to make him understand her just a bit. Like how she wanted to trust him, but he was taking control of her heart too fast, and she was deathly afraid he would steal it and tear it into a thousand scraps, leaving her empty as a shell.

She could barely look at him, she was so embarrassed of what he must think of her. The woman who really wanted to be loved, but who freaked out the second someone tried to break through her carefully constructed brick wall. Or bra.

"I don't even know what to say right now," she admitted.

"And not having anything to say says an awful lot, don't you think?" He didn't sound angry. Just tired and frustrated, but not mad. "I think the ball is officially in your court at this point. I'll follow your lead."

They stood by the door and stared at each other. Why couldn't she just take this chance with him? What was the worst thing that could happen? She'd have her heart broken, but she'd been through that before and lived. But this thing with Matthew felt different, and it had nothing to do with him being younger. Age didn't even seem like a factor in this, even though she had fixated on it. Matthew was unlike any man she had dated, and she couldn't deny that some sort of string was tied between them, and it kept pulling them closer and closer. All she had to do was take that one final step into his arms. To just toss that ball in his direction so he could catch it.

But she didn't. She was chicken shit. And really, really disappointed in herself.

"Goodnight, Jules. Drive carefully," he said, kissing the top of her head and opening the door for her.

"Okay, see you." She turned away from him, swallowing the words she couldn't say, feeling the ache and disappointment as they slid down her throat.

He closed the door with a soft click, and she hesitated before heading down the stairs, hoping he might open the door again. But he said the ball was now in her court. Which meant he probably wasn't going to come out to get her. Still, she waited a few more hopeful minutes, and then sat cross-legged on the hallway rug, wrote a list of songs on the back of a CVS receipt, and shoved it under his door.

🎸 SEVEN

Matthew

"Gracie is out of fucking tune, man. Get your shit to-gether," John snapped, noodling on the synthesizer. The one Klein had bought him. The one he barely knew how to play.

"Screw you," Matthew shot back, and grabbed another beer.

"And stop drinking during practice. You're crap when you drink," Coop added, tightening his cymbals. "Why the fuck do you have that acoustic out anyway? That's not what Klein wants."

"Is there anything else we can do for fucking Klein?" He tossed the empty beer bottle on the worn-out carpet and tried to tune Gracie, but she refused to cooperate.

Either that, or he'd starting losing motor skills. That could happen after a six-pack. He accidentally dropped the guitar, a hollow thud echoing through the practice space.

"Enough. Group meeting. *Again.*" John motioned Matthew and Coop over to the couch.

Shit. Matthew hated when John called this kumbaya crap. He didn't want to talk. He just wanted to drink. And kick the shit out of that synthesizer. And kiss Jules again.

Jules, who he hadn't heard from in two weeks. That woman had a nasty habit of disappearing. Well, could he blame her? She obviously had control issues, and there he was, trying to mold her into something she wasn't, and trying to take her goddamn bra off the first time they kissed. He was a fucking idiot.

You waited with a woman like her, even if every cell in your body screamed out to make love to her. You needed to trust each other first, and he hadn't done anything to gain hers yet. Not by a long shot.

John sat with his arms draped across the back of the ripped couch. Coop was sitting upside down, his head hanging over the edge of the cushions, whacking his legs with his drumsticks.

Matthew stood, arms crossed, waiting for the onslaught.

John spoke first. "What the fuck is wrong with you? I thought we agreed we were going to at least try this. And now you're going all Bob Goddamn Miserable Dylan and shit on us?"

Coop nodded in agreement, his Adam's apple

bobbing up and down. Matthew wanted to smack it with those drumsticks.

"I can't do it. I'm all set with this shit." Where had he heard those words before? Julia's voice echoed in his head. Christ, he really wanted to see her and somehow make things right again.

But right now he needed to deal with this Seymour Klein bullshit. Klein had called to request a Joyride demo on the night after Jules had walked out of his apartment. Matthew felt like he'd been waiting his whole goddamn life for that call. But his excitement lasted for about a millisecond, because Klein had his own ideas for Joyride.

That asshole wanted to scrape the marrow right out of the band's bones, leaving nothing more than a sissy skeleton. Soulless synthesizers and tinny electric drums. Shiny suits. *Hair gel.* They'd been trying for two weeks to write some new songs for him. All of it was shit, and with each passing day, Matthew grew more and more jaded. He just wanted to play *his* music, not what someone else thought he should be playing. No way was he going to show the world an album full of crap. Not when he'd worked so hard.

Coop tossed his sticks in the air and caught them. "*Can't do it?* We talked about this already. Now you say you can't fucking do it?"

John blew smoke rings. "If quitting my shitty day job depends on tweaking our songs with a few synths, I think we should at least give it a shot."

"It's not just that, and you fucking know it. You're fooling yourselves if you think we can just change everything about who we are. Tweak, my ass. It's not about money. Do you really want to sell a piece of your soul for a paycheck?"

"You want this as bad as the rest of us do, Matthew. Don't pull that suffering for art crap on me now," John sneered. "All you do is talk about how much you hate your job. How badly you want to make it. Well, this is your ticket out. This is what we have to do to get what we've always wanted."

Coop chimed in. "We're never going to get the attention of someone like Klein again. This is it, man. Our one shot. Don't flake out on us now."

But Matthew didn't know what he wanted anymore. When he dreamed about making it to the top, it never started like this. His blood pumped because of music. The one thing that got him out of goddamn bed every day was music. And now he would have to cheapen himself? Lie to himself? Just to get a *shot* at becoming famous?

He headed for the door. "I'm out. And don't forget for one fucking second that Joyride is *my* band. I asked the two of you to be in it because I thought you had the same vision as me. If you want to be a foppy bunch of airheads just to make money, be my guest. But you're not doing it under my band name. *No way.*"

He slammed the door and headed for home where a bottle of tequila and a list of songs waited for him. He was going to listen to that miserable, beautiful list for the hundredth time. He didn't think his heart could take it, but he wanted the pain anyway. He had to hand it to Jules. The girl knew how to break a heart through vinyl. Kate Bush. The Cure. U2. The Smiths. The Police. And some seventies tearjerkers like Badfinger and Todd Rundgren.

He studied the lyrics, trying to decipher the message she had sent through songs that slayed his heart with beauty. Some lush and sweeping. Some melancholy dirges with voices barely above a whisper, choking out the lyrics until their breath ran out. Each listen left him exhausted. Left him wanting her more. Was she saying goodbye? Was she writing him a musical love letter? What the fuck was he supposed to do with all this emotional baggage she had left at his door?

It had been two weeks. Two long weeks of no lunchtime visits, yet he still made her sandwich, just in case. She'd skipped their last two lessons, but he still waited with Gracie on the couch, coffee made, music books out. He'd even made her an easy-to-follow fret chart that he hoped might help her to enjoy practice. He was willing to do anything to help her play. To not be so frustrated. To trust that he wanted the best for her, musically and emotionally. But most of all, he didn't want her to give up on herself.

And now, Matthew wasn't going to get that coveted contract, his band was probably on the outs, and he'd lost the only girl who made his entire body sing. The only girl he'd ever met who understood what it meant to live with music in your DNA.

What the hell did he have left?

He downed his third shot and stretched out on the rug, the alcohol spreading quickly through his heavy limbs, the music filling his head. God, he wished she was lying here beside him. He didn't know what he would say to her to change anything, but just having her in the same room would be enough for now.

Buzz. Buzz. Buzz.

His head throbbed. Who the fuck was ringing his bell at this hour? Probably that drunk, Sam, from the second floor. He was forever losing his keys. Well, he could wait a little longer. If Matthew even lifted his head up an inch, he was going to throw up.

Buzz. Buzz. Buzz.

For fuck's sake. Couldn't he bother someone else? Matthew was tired of always being the nice guy in the building. The one who helped carry groceries and shoveled the walkway when the landlord got too busy.

He was fucking done with all of it.

Buzz. Buzz. Buzz.

Jesus H. Christ. He rolled over, ignoring the stiffness in his body from sleeping on the floor, and stumbled to the door, hitting the buzzer over and over so he wouldn't have to do it again in case Sam was too drunk to figure out how a fucking doorknob worked. Then he shuffled to his bedroom and fell heavily on his unmade bed.

Knock. Knock. Knock.

He bunched his pillow and put it over his head. He wanted to yell, "Go away," but even the idea of opening his mouth was too exhausting. He wished whoever was knocking at the door would just come the fuck in and whack him on the head with a hammer. Anything to put an end to his misery.

🎸 EIGHT

Julia

Julia smelled bacon and heard the grind of coffee beans.

She sat up quickly, wondering where the hell she was before she recognized the pattern on the hallway carpet. Singing and humming floated out from the other side of the door, and the day before came back to her in fuzzy bits and pieces.

Andrew and Kate had taken her out to dinner. Well, they ate their dinner. She drank hers. She hadn't had that much to drink in years. Maybe ever.

Earlier that same day, Kate had stood before her desk, clicking that goddamn pen again. "We are all going out for dinner tonight, and if you say no, I'm quitting.

How about that? And kudos to you for finally trusting James. It's about time, you freak."

"Whatever, it wasn't that big of a deal," Julia mumbled, studying the proofs that all looked the same. Why was she in the ad business anyway? She spent her days making everyone else look perfect. Taking care of their every whim. Who was going to take care of *her*?

Certainly not Matthew. Maybe he would have. Who knows? But not now. Not after that disaster on the couch.

Still, she had hoped he might get in touch, thinking that the list she had slipped under his door might prompt him to reach out. Wasn't that putting the ball in his court? She had put her soul on that paper, digging deep into all the songs that defined her life, the good and the bad. She regretted leaving him the way she did.

For the past two weeks, she had been thinking non-stop about what Matthew had said to her, to the point where it started to affect her ability to concentrate. Kate kept finding mistakes in her correspondence. Julia read page after page of copy and couldn't remember any of it when she was done. What was happening to her? She was losing her grip and couldn't handle her workload any longer. She knew what she had to do, even if the thought of it set her teeth on edge. It took a good bit of soul searching before she finally decided to hand off two of her most important accounts to James. If she didn't, she was going to let the clients down, and that was not an option for her, or the agency.

James had seemed surprised when she called him into her office and handed the files over to him.

"Is this some sort of joke?" he asked as he looked through the files. "These are our biggest accounts. Our biggest money makers."

She leaned back in her chair and twirled her Mont Blanc pen. "Yup. And I'm too busy right now to deal with them."

James cleared his throat and placed the files back on her desk. "Can I just ask what's prompted this? You haven't been exactly keen on letting me take the reins. I mean, I know you're still vetting me, but this seems, dare I say, out of character for you. Really, what's the catch?"

Julia laughed, mostly at herself. Good for James for having the balls to question her motives. She knew she had hired this guy for a reason. "I'm not setting you up to fail, if that's what you mean. Maybe I haven't been too vocal about it, but I think you're doing tremendous work here. So I'm giving you an opportunity to shine. Of course, if you don't want it, I understand."

"Of course I want it. I'm just surprised. And really grateful. I won't let you down, Julia."

She wagged her finger at him. "You better not. All I ask is that you keep me in the loop, okay?"

"Will do. Of course. And thank you, again."

After he left her office, she let out the breath she'd been holding. She had taken some of Matthew's advice and let go, *and she didn't die*. She knew James would do a good job, and that her business wasn't going to fall apart, even if he made a mistake or two. Still, this was a major step for her. She wondered what Matthew would think of what she had just done.

Christ, she missed him. She wanted those soft lips on hers again. Wanted to be back in his cozy apartment eating grilled cheese and making out on his couch.

Kate sat down with a thud in the chair across from her desk, the one that James had occupied only a day ago. "It's a huge deal, giving over those accounts. But deny it if that makes you feel better. So, are we on for dinner? Andrew misses you. And he wants to know how those guitar lessons are going. Wants to know when we get a concert," Kate chuckled, still clicking that infernal pen. Julia made a mental note to never order clicking pens again. "What is up with these lessons, by the way? You've dodged every one of my questions about them. Don't you like playing with Matthew?" She batted her eyelashes.

Julia shifted in her seat. "Don't be ridiculous."

Click. Click. Clickity click.

"Ha! I *knew* you were hiding something from me. You can't even look me in the eye. Tell me everything. And don't you dare leave out any details."

"There's nothing to tell, Katherine Jane."

Kate hated being called by her full name and Julia made a mental note to use it more often during times like this. And to throw out all the clicking pens.

"Fine, be that way." Kate pouted. "But you're not getting out of dinner tonight and that's final. Be there at seven, or we will come to your apartment, bare-ass naked, and embarrass you in front of all your snobby condo neighbors. Got it? And believe me, no one wants to see Andrew naked. He's really hairy."

"Why do I even pay you to be my assistant?"

"Because I'm awesome and rad and can type a mile a minute. Plus, I'm totally rocking this Madonna outfit today. Oh, and no one else could put up with your seesaw moods the way I do. Florentina's at seven. Or, you know, naked me and *hairy*, naked Andrew running around the condo complex."

Julia went to dinner. All food looked unappetizing, even though it was her favorite restaurant. At least they had top shelf alcohol. She ordered a bourbon. And then another.

"Slow it down there, champ. You didn't have lunch today," Kate warned.

"Matthew tells me you haven't shown up for a couple of lessons," Andrew mentioned, looking through the menu. His mohawk was an electric blue today. Somehow, he pulled it off. The snooty patrons gave him dirty looks, but he didn't give a shit, a trait Julia admired. She would *love* to not give a shit for once.

Julia choked at his comment, liquid fire in her chest. "Oh, did he now?" So, he had been asking about her. Why did her heart feel like someone had hooked it up to a generator? It beat against her rib cage with a fierce thump.

Kate had a knowing smirk on her face. Julia raised an eyebrow at her.

"Yeah, he called me a couple of weeks ago with some great news. Joyride could get signed soon. Seymour Klein listened to their demo and asked them to send some new songs along. This is huge."

"That's great." Julia tried to sound like she didn't care, but she did. She really did. This was what Matthew wanted, and she wanted to be able to share that happiness with him. She wished he had told her, but he probably had too much pride to chase after the woman that had led him on, and then rejected him. Good for him. She deserved to be left out.

Andrew continued on, unaware that Julia wanted to crawl under the table and hide. "I guess it was a bad time to take lessons with him, yeah? If they get signed, he won't need to teach anymore. A band that good? They'll be raking in the dough."

The image of Matthew and his dimple on the cover of *Rolling Stone* or *Melody Maker* made her heart seize. Matthew could very well give Sting a ride for his money. Kate had been right when she said he sounded like him. Shit, Matthew even *looked* like Sting, and like an idiot, she had stopped that gorgeous man from kissing her. Stopped him from making love to her. She really needed to get her head put on straight.

And *what if* Matthew became famous? Julia would be nothing but a distant memory. Just some old lady who lusted after him and quit after two lessons because she was too embarrassed to fail, too embarrassed to go for what her heart wanted. Regret seeped through her body along with the alcohol, making her numb.

"So, um, he must be pretty happy, "Julia said. "He did mention that all he ever wanted was for the band to go national."

Andrew spoke through a mouthful of bread. "When we were at school together, I thought he'd end up being a teacher, you know? He was always helping other people with their lessons. He just had this knack for it. People really *listened* to him. I mean, with the talent he's got? He was going to be top of the class. No question. I always felt bad about the shit he had to deal with."

"What shit?" Julia asked. Matthew had mentioned something to her about being on his own at a young age, but she had been too caught up in her own shit to even bother to find out why.

"His scholarship money ran out after one year, and he didn't have anyone to help him out once it was gone. Buckley was his entire life, and after that was taken away, he checked out for a while. Stopped talking to people. I was really worried about him. He was, like, *morose*."

"That's so sad." Kate looked like she was about to cry.

"That's terrible," Julia added, tears forming. She thought about Matthew's apartment, how everything in it seemed old and worn, yet comfortable. Nothing extra. She hadn't even noticed a TV. How hard he must have worked for all of it. Her insides ached at the thought of him struggling. Yet he seemed so happy, so comfortable with exactly who he was. It made her fall in love with him even more, which was ridiculous because she'd already ruined things between them.

"Yeah, but a lot of teachers really missed him, and felt bad, so they helped him out by sending students to him for tutoring. It didn't pay a ton, but he was really goddamn good at it. I kept telling him to teach full-time, open up his own school, but he insisted it would never work. Plus, he already had the management job and was finally making decent money. When Joyride happened, he set all his hopes on the band. Looks like it's gonna work out after all. I'm so fucking happy for him. No one deserves it more than him."

"He is a great teacher," Julia admitted. She was just an exceptionally crappy student.

"The band's been practicing like crazy. I stopped by awhile back to see what they were up to. But I gotta say, something bothered me. Matthew looks like shit. They all do."

"But they should be happy," Kate chirped. "They're going to be famous! I'm totally going to become a groupie. Julia, be a groupie with me. Pinky swear with me right this instant. I get Coop. You need to like someone else. We can't both like the same one." She stuck her pinky in Julia's face.

"It's like I'm not even here sometimes," said Andrew.

Julia brushed Kate off. "I'm not twelve. I'm not pinky swearing with you."

Kate said something under her breath. Something about Julia and Matthew sitting and kissing in a tree. Julia stuck her tongue out at her and it felt like pins and needles. So did the rest of her.

"Anyway, something's going on with him. I'll probably stop by later and see how he's doing. Care to join me, Jules?" Andrew winked at her.

"Me? Why would I want to do that?" Julia sputtered, hardly believing that Andrew could be so cheeky. Obviously, he knew something was going on and had been involved from the start. She could only imagine the things Matthew had told him about her. Embarrassing things. Hurtful things. But would Matthew do that? She didn't think he would, but after three bourbons, she didn't know much.

"No reason," he smirked. "Ouch, Jesus, what the hell, Kate? My shin!"

"*Andrew*, leave Julia alone."

He covered his hand with his heart. "What? What am I doing now? I haven't said anything!"

Julia downed the rest of her bourbon. She rarely drank, so it hit her hard. The buzz took that edge off, the one she had been standing on for what felt like forever. She was so tired of thinking about her boring, carefully constructed life.

"Tell me something, Katherine Jane," she slurred. Wait, was she slurring? Her mouth felt weird.

"This ought to be interesting. You only call me that when you're annoyed with me."

"I'm old and boring, right? Do you find me old and boring?" She desperately needed to know if everyone else felt the same way Matthew did about her. But didn't Matthew like her? Didn't he want to kiss her? She really, really wanted to kiss Matthew and do all the dirty things with him.

"I'm not going to answer that when you're tipsy. Order some food. Andrew, order something for Julia."

"I knew it. I'm too tough. No fun." She slapped her hand on the table. "I'm a control freak. Just say it. Julia is a crazy control freak. C.O.N.T.R.L. Wait, let me do that again. C.O…"

"Nope, not gonna say it. And apparently we aren't going to spell it, either."

"I can be fun, right? You know. *You know it*," Julia

hiccupped and poked Kate in the chest with her index finger.

"A barrel of monkeys. Now I think we should order some food. How about some food?"

Julia tried to stand up. She needed to pee. But there was no floor.

"Whoa!" Andrew saved her from an embarrassing face plant. "I think someone has had enough."

"You have no idea what I need, *Andrew*." She tried to push him away, but it felt like pushing into a concrete wall. "Shit, I'm sorry. I'm just… I'm just…"

"Drunk is the word you are looking for."

"Yea, that, *Katherine Jane*." She poked Kate in the arm. "Bingo. You get a raise. No, I'm going to fire you." Julia couldn't stop her mouth from saying things. "Do you think I should fire her, Andrew?"

Kate took her by the wrist. "Maybe we should just go home. I think you'll feel better at home. You can fire me tomorrow. How does that sound?"

She felt so fuzzy. "And I'm shit at C. C suuucksss. Ask Matthew. Matthew thinks I'm terrible. Awful."

"Okay, that's enough, sweetie. Let's go home." Andrew sounded muted, like he was speaking from a fish bowl. Then she was walking. And then maybe she was in a car. Someone was helping her up the stairs. The big man with big blue hair. And the pretty girl with blonde curls and a nose ring helped her to her bedroom. Some people could be so nice.

Matthew's sweatshirt was on her bed. She put it on and smelled it. Clean laundry. *Mmm.*

She crawled under the covers, saying something

over and over, but she couldn't remember what. Why couldn't she remember anything?

"Of course you're in love with him, you idiot," said the pretty girl. "But you're telling the wrong person, drunkie." Or at least that's what Julia thought she heard, but she couldn't be sure because the big blue man put a blanket over her, and then, nothing.

NINE

Matthew

The sun streaming through the window burned holes into Matthew's retinas. Jesus Christ, what time was it? He jumped up and looked at the clock. Nine. He still had time to get ready for his first lesson of the day.

His head felt like it might pop right off his shoulders. Fucking tequila. The asshole of all liquors. He was never drinking it again.

Outside his window, the leaves were falling. Bright orange and yellow swirls in the air. He found it hard to believe that something dead could be so beautiful. The tree shed its skin, slept for a while, and came back lush and vibrant again. Its death wasn't permanent, only a phase to be repeated over and over.

How many times did he have to die before he got it right?

Shit. He was getting too deep and depressing for a Saturday morning. He needed strong coffee and a shower, and then he could start to think straight. About Joyride. About Julia. So many fucking loose ends that he just wanted to somehow tie up.

He took a quick shower, washing off the grime of yesterday, and then got breakfast ready. Measure the beans. Grind the beans. Boil the water. He knew Julia had watched him carefully that first day. He loved to make things for her. To show her he cared in small ways, but she didn't seem to want anything else from him.

Grease. He wanted grease, too. He put the bacon on the griddle and while it sizzled, he cued up some jazz. The Sidewinder always got him smiling.

He heard a knock on his door over Lee Morgan's cheery trumpet. Ben liked to show up early because Matthew had coffee waiting for him. Ben's mom didn't like him to drink it. She thought it made him more hyper than usual. And, man, hyper didn't even *begin* to describe Ben. But Matthew found that coffee helped Ben focus better. He was lucky if he got Ben to sit still for their hour lesson, but they'd been working together for over three months now, and he had made some improvements. Matthew liked to think he had a little bit to do with that.

But when he opened the door, it wasn't just Ben standing there.

Someone else was there, too.

Julia.

He fought the strong urge to gather her up in his arms and kiss her entire face. But he had to play calm, cool and collected, even while his head swam with all the good and bad reasons she may have for showing up at his door.

"Hey Ben, good morning. And who's this lovely lady you brought along today?"

"Dude, I didn't bring her. She was sleeping outside your door." Ben looked at Julia. "Are you homeless or something?"

Her eyes and nose were red, and her hair wild. She wore his sweatshirt.

"I'm not homeless. I just got... locked out," Julia stuttered.

"Locked out infers that you have a key. Did I give you a key?" Matthew smirked. God help him, he was having fun watching her squirm, even though he was pretty sure she hated every second of it.

"Man, I don't know what's going on between you two, but I smell java and I'm going in. Looks like you got some serious women problems," joked Ben as he pushed his way past Matthew.

"Funny, Matthew, real funny," said Julia. "I've been here since six this morning. I must have fallen asleep waiting for you to open the door."

Matthew crossed his arms and leaned against the doorjamb. "Why didn't you just knock?"

"I did knock. At least I think I did."

"I can think of easier ways to return my sweatshirt."

"Are you going to let me in?" she demanded, clearly

frustrated. "I'm starving and that bacon smell is driving me nuts. And I kinda need to use the bathroom."

"Oh, so you want me to make you food, do you? This isn't the Sandwich Factory, Whole Wheat."

She put her hand on her hip and stuck it out. "No. I don't want you to cook for me."

Christ, he had missed her. Her sass. Her hair. Her voice. "Wow, that's too bad. Because all these months that I've been making you lunch?"

"Yes?" she asked, tapping her foot.

He leaned towards her and whispered in her ear. "All I *really* wanted to do was make you breakfast."

He had wanted to say that to her at work every goddamn time she thanked him for making her a sandwich. He was glad he'd waited for the perfect moment to shock her with it, and the stunned look on her face told him he'd done exactly that.

"Ben, enough with the coffee. Leave some for Julia," Matthew called out. "Seriously, your mother is going to kill me if you're bouncing off the walls when she comes to get you."

"He's not old enough to drink coffee. What is he, twelve?" asked Julia, following him into the kitchen.

"Actually, he's fifteen, but he's got some learning issues. I don't know, he likes to be here and I like having him. I actually get him to smile once in a while, and I get the feeling he doesn't do that very often," Matthew said, motioning toward the stove full of food. "There's plenty if you want some. I've got this lesson for the next hour, but you're more than welcome to hang out. If you want."

She swiped a piece of bacon off the stove. "Do you mind if I come in there with you and listen?"

"Sure, that's cool by me. But I guess we should check in with Ben first. He's having some trouble with this new song and I'm not sure if he'll want an audience. He's super hard on himself."

Matthew looked her in the eye when he said that, hoping his point sunk in even a little bit. She looked down at her Converse.

Ben sat on the couch, strumming his guitar and reading off a hand-written music sheet. He sounded off-tune and out of rhythm, but kept on playing. Matthew hoped Julia took some notice.

"Ben, my homeless friend, Julia, would like to sit in on your lesson. You know, just to watch. She's one of my students, too. That okay with you?"

"Whatever floats your boat, dude."

"We've still got a lot of work to do on this song before the concert, so let's get practicing."

"Don't remind me," Ben said, "I've only got six months to try not to suck donkey balls."

As Matthew got Ben settled, Julia took off her shoes and curled up on a chair on the other side of the living room. Matthew felt slightly self-conscious at first, but got wrapped up in the lesson quickly. Ben's hour was his most difficult, but also his favorite. He loved the proud gleam in Ben's eye when he could set his frustration aside and focus long enough to play a chord correctly. With Matthew's patience, Ben had been showing slow improvements. He refused to give up, even when he was having an off day, like today.

Ben trusted Matthew and Matthew had faith in Ben. That's what it was all about.

Matthew wished Julia could do that, too. He knew she could do anything she put her mind to, if only she would just give herself a break and trust him to help her stop trying to be so damn perfect. There was no such thing as perfect in his world. You did the best you could with what you had, and that was enough.

As Ben played through his lesson, Matthew stole glances at Julia. He wanted to tell her that she'd never looked more beautiful than she did in this moment. Hair crazy. Mascara under her eyes. Clothes disheveled. Just like the day she showed up on his doorstep, soaking wet. She didn't need to be anything other than herself for him. All the rest didn't matter. The clothes. The makeup. And her age, especially. How could he get her to see that she was already enough, just as she was?

"Wow, man, I bit today," Ben laughed at the end of the lesson, putting his guitar into its beat up case. "Sorry, man."

"Well, you were better than last week, so that's something to be happy about."

He could see Julia move in her chair, and Matthew knew she was listening.

"Maybe I shouldn't be in the concert," Ben lamented.

"So you're just going to back out now? After all the work you've put into this? We still have six months."

"Yeah, but you heard me. I'm having trouble with the first chorus and I can't get it perfect. My parents are going to be there. And that girl. The one I told you about?"

"Amy? How could I forget? You talk about her every week."

"If I fuck up in front of her, she's going to dump me," he said.

"If she does that, then let her. She's not worth it. Just go out there and do your best. As your teacher, that's all I ask. Quitting isn't even an option right now. I won't let you." Matthew ruffled Ben's hair. "Just keep practicing the stuff we went over today and I promise by the concert you will sound far less sucky."

"Don't tell my mom about the coffee," Ben said as Matthew let him out. "She'll kill me."

They high-fived. "Never, man. Musicians' honor."

Matthew closed the door and leaned his forehead against it. He needed a moment to compose himself before going back in there with Jules. He'd worried through Ben's entire lesson that she'd come here to quit her lessons or end whatever was happening between them. He didn't know what the fuck was going on in his life right now. Shit, he didn't even know if he had a band anymore.

He found her curled up into a tight little ball and asleep on the chair. Julia slept like she lived - closed up and inward. Rather than wake her up, he grabbed Gracie, sat down on the rug and began to play softly. He had been trying for over two weeks to convey his feelings through chords and melodies, putting a whole group of new material together, like Julia had with her list. Melodies were haunting him and he had played them for the guys last night, but acoustic wasn't what Klein wanted from Joyride. He wanted soulless drivel.

Fucking Klein.

He plucked and strummed, getting lost in the sound, his fingers taking over, the notes swirling around him just like those beautiful leaves this morning. Dying and coming back to life. He could start over on his own. He didn't need a band. All he knew was that he would die if he stopped playing, and that wasn't a goddamn option.

"That is the most beautiful thing I've ever heard."

Matthew stopped mid-strum, hearing the squeak of chair springs as she sat up. "Please don't stop on my account."

"It's nothing really."

But it wasn't nothing. Not at all. It was everything he felt about her condensed into a three-minute love song.

"Is that a new Joyride song?" she asked, wrapping her arms around her knees.

Matthew plucked and tuned Gracie. "It's a new song. But not for Joyride. As of last night, Joyride doesn't exist anymore. I quit."

She lifted her eyebrows in surprise. "You what?"

"My band. My name. If they want to go on without me, that's their choice."

"But last night, Andrew said that Klein…"

Matthew cut her off. "Andrew doesn't know everything. Klein is a snake in the grass. Wants to turn us into some techno pussy band. Well, I'm not gonna do it."

"What about Coop and John?"

"What about them? If they want to wear makeup and white jazz shoes, they can be my guest, but my name will be nowhere near that shit."

"Wow. So what are you going to do now?" She got

off the chair and joined him on the rug. She smelled like bourbon, flowers and sleep. He wanted to kiss her all over and then start again, but instead he stared at his guitar.

"Start a new band, I guess. I don't know. I haven't had much time to think about it. I guess pick up more hours at the shop now that I'm not gigging or practicing anymore."

"That's the last thing you should do. You hate it there."

Matthew ran his hands through his already disheveled hair. "Okay, Whole Wheat, why don't you tell me what I should do? Do you want to hire me? I could serenade your workforce for a small fee."

She took Gracie out of his arms, and tried to strum C. The sound hurt his ears. God, she really was terrible. "You know what I think? I think you should be a teacher."

"Yes, because I'm so *good* at it," he joked. "You're well on your way to being the next Jimmy Page because of my mad teaching skills."

"Don't use me as an example. Look at Ben. The kid worships the ground you walk on and you refuse to give up on him."

Matthew grabbed a pillow and tucked it behind his head. "He's really trying. And he's a good kid. As long as he keeps practicing and showing up, what more can I ask of him?"

"Well, I'd say that's pretty admirable."

"I don't know how admirable I am, but thank you."

She cleared her throat and looked down. He knew

what was coming next. He braced for it and told himself that he hadn't known her that long, so if she vanished from his life, he'd get over it. He'd die a little inside, just like those leaves, but maybe he'd come back stronger for it.

But he was feeding himself a line of bullshit. He wouldn't get over her and he didn't want her to go anywhere. He wished she would just sit on this floor forever, in his sweatshirt, and kiss the living hell out of him. He wondered if she had that red lace bra again, and then felt bad for even thinking that because it wasn't just sex he wanted from Julia. He wanted all of her. But she was incapable of letting anyone have it.

She still wasn't saying anything, and he couldn't stand the silence. His nerves were frayed. "So, how did you end up asleep in my hallway?" He picked at fuzz on the carpet. "I'm assuming you really needed to tell me something?"

"Yeah, that. That's a good story. Well, I got pretty drunk last night with Andrew and Kate. Wait, let me rephrase that. I got drunk. They did not, thank goodness. I think I was well on my way to making a total fool of myself and they had my back."

"A drunk Julia. Now that I can't even imagine. Sorry I missed it. But I was too busy having my own drunken pity party."

"Because of Joyride?"

"Because of a lot of things," Matthew admitted.

"I guess it's safe to say that I'm one of those things." Julia stood up and walked over to the other side of the room, looking at the albums strewn about. She picked them up one by one, a look of recognition on her face. "Wait, these are all the…"

"The songs you gave me," he finished. "Stellar list, by the way. Like arrows to the heart. Thanks for that."

She slumped her shoulders and rubbed at her forehead. "Matthew, I'm sorry and I don't even know what I'm apologizing for."

"You still haven't answered my question."

"Why did I come here? I wish I knew."

"Well that's a sucky answer," he laughed nervously.

"It's just that… I was sitting alone in my condo, half drunk and all I could think about was being here." She motioned to the records, the couch and his guitars, and then at him. "I came back because of how I feel when I'm with you, which scares the crap out of me. And also for the fact that *no one* in my twenty years of dating has *ever* made me coffee before, never mind a perfect grilled cheese."

He stood up and walked over to her. "No one has ever cooked for you before?"

"Nope. Not even one measly Pop-Tart."

He rested his chin on the top of her head and felt her sigh heavily. "Not for nothing, but who the fuck have you been dating, Whole Wheat?"

"All the wrong people, evidently." He heard the catch in her voice.

He threaded his hands through the hair at the nape of her neck and she pressed in closer to him. God, he had missed touching her. Smelling her. Even though his nerves were on edge, he could begin to feel his body relaxing the closer he got to her. "I'm afraid to ask, but am I now lumped into that group of wrong people?"

"No, and that's part of the problem."

"I don't want to be something you need to handle, Jules. I don't want to be a problem," Matthew whispered. "But if you can't just let go, I'm afraid that's all I'm ever going to be."

She shook her head from side to side against his chest. "This is all too much," she said, her voice muffled by his T-shirt. "Shit, I suck. I know I have this ridiculous need to make sure nothing bad happens. And I have absolutely no idea how to deal with any of this. I can't get a grip. It's a scary feeling."

"If you figure out a way to get a grip, let me in on it."

"But everything seems so easy for you. Nothing bothers you."

He wrapped his arms around her and pulled her closer. "I'm scared to death every day, but the difference is that I say fuck you to my fear, and do it anyway. You know, like when I kissed you for the first time. Do you know how overjoyed I was that you didn't smack my face?"

"Oh, Matthew," she sighed. "I've wanted to kiss you since the second I saw you."

"*Now* she tells me."

"But my wheels come off when I'm with you. And that frightens me. Because, well, because…"

He tipped her face up to his and looked into her eyes. They were red-rimmed. He hated that he was causing her so much pain when all he wanted to do was just make love to her if she'd let him. "Because why?"

She looked away from him. Here it was. She was going to drop the gavel and his heart was going to split apart like an atom, leaving a hole where his chest should be.

"I'm no good at this. Relationships. I'm about as good at being a girlfriend as I am at playing guitar. And what has me messed up is that I really like you. Like, *really, really* like you, but I know how it's going to end before it even starts. I'm going to try and control you, and then you're going to leave me, and I'm just going to be left sitting in my condo, old and heartbroken."

"Wow, that's a mouthful of misery. And very creative."

"See what I mean?" she declared, a lone tear glinting at the edge of her eyelash.

"Julia Powers. Listen to me. You're absolutely right. You probably will try to control me. You already do. But guess what? I've got way too much goddamn pride to let you do that. So I'll push back. And you'll learn to give a little and so will I, because that's how this relationship thing works."

The tear fell and rolled down her flushed cheek.

"And guess what else? I have no idea what's going to happen. I can't predict the future. But what I *do* know is that I feel good when I'm with you. Fuck age. Fuck all that. I just know you make me smile and I want to be near you all the time. Have ever since you told me how to make a damn sandwich. And that's the only truth I can give you right now."

More tears rolled until his sweatshirt was stained dark gray.

"Do you want to be with me, Julia? Do you? Because if you say yes, I'm going to try real hard to make up for the twenty years' worth of assholes you dated."

"And if I say no?" She looked up at him with those golden eyes that bore through him like a laser.

His last bits of hope crumbled to dust as he swallowed the lump in his throat. "I actually didn't think that far ahead."

"Well, that's a really good thing."

He felt like he might soar to the sun. Relief coursed through his entire body and he picked her up and carried her into his bedroom, placing her gently on his bed. He wasn't letting her go. Not this time. If she freaked out and tried to leave again, he was going to attach himself to her ankles. She'd have to drag him out with her.

"Whole Wheat, are we okay?"

She nodded.

"Good," he said, a twinkle in his eye. "Because I want my sweatshirt back. Right now."

🎸 TEN

Matthew

She raised her arms, the green light he had been waiting for. Matthew grabbed the bottom of that goddamn sweatshirt and slid it up, over and off. Ah, the red bra again. She watched him intently as he scraped his T-shirt off and threw it to the side. He pulled his jeans off and tossed them carelessly onto the floor.

They knelt before one another on his bed.

"Impressive," Julia said as she ran her palms over his chest and abs. "I always wondered what you looked like under your work uniform." She squeezed his biceps and forearms. "Guitar arms."

He peppered her face and neck with soft kisses. "I've been wondering about your underwear since you walked in the door the first time. Does she wear bikinis?

Calvin Kleins? Nothing? And the answer is…" Matthew started at her shoulders and slid his palms slowly down to her thighs and back again, gently pushing her leggings down. "And the answer is…"

"Wrong. A thong," she giggled, pushing him onto his back and stretching her body along the length of his. The only pieces of material between them her lace and his striped boxers. He caressed her from shoulders to waist, delighting in finally being this close to her.

"I suppose I should tell you up front that, well, I haven't done this in a while."

"That makes the two of us." He hoped his admission made her feel better, or at least took away any fear she might have of him being the kind of guy who slept around a lot.

"Funny, I always imagined you with a lot of women. At the same time."

"I'm sorry to disappoint you. But now that you bring it up, that does sound like a lot of fun."

She playfully slapped his arm. "Cut it out."

He pulled her closer. If there was a way he could crawl underneath her skin and live there forever, he would. "I'm kind of a one-woman guy."

He molded himself to her body until it was impossible to tell where one ended and the other began. Her breasts pressed against his chest and he wrapped his legs around her waist, flipping them over until she spread out beneath him.

He caressed and kissed her breasts, licking her nipples through the delicate lace material, delighting in her sighs and moans.

"Let me look at you." His voice was rough with emotion. He raised himself up on his arms and began to pull the straps of her bra down.

She covered her breasts. Why was she closing down on him again?

"Hey, hey, what's wrong?" he said, stroking her hair. "I just want to see all of you. Well, I don't want to. I'm kinda *dying* to."

She looked him right in the eyes. "This is it, Matthew. This lace is the last bit of wall I've got. The last brick. After that, I'll be wide open to you."

"Isn't that the point of what we're doing here? I trust you with my heart, and you trust me with yours. That's how this works." He placed his hand on her wildly beating heart.

"I'm trying really hard with this trust thing. You probably won't believe this, but I actually gave some important work to a colleague. I thought I was going to pass out after I did it."

"And?" He ran his hands up and down her goosebumped arms. He just wanted to make her warm and keep her safe. To let her know that no matter what she feared was coming around the corner, they would deal with it. Together. Like a team. Like a band. And speaking of bands, he needed stop being a hypocrite and connect with his own and see if they could compromise somehow. "Well, tell me. What happened?"

"Nothing. I lived."

"See? That pesky, brilliant brain of yours…" He stopped talking to kiss his way down her neck and collarbone. And this time, when he snapped open the front clip of her bra, she let him, never taking her eyes off of his. "…it really needs to take a vacation."

"I'm beginning to realize that," she said, relaxing under his touch.

"God, you're so beautiful." He took all of her in. Her creamy, pale skin. Curves, dips, hills and valleys. "And I'm not going to lie, Jules. I really want to make love to you. If you'll let me. But if it's too soon, I understand. I just… goddamn, I just want to feel all of you at once."

Matthew knew the feeling of getting lost in a song, of having it wrap around you and take you to places you had no idea existed within yourself. But that didn't even compare to making love with Julia.

He wanted to bury himself inside her and get lost in her music, to ride out their blissful melody through chorus and verse, crashing solos and pounding drumbeats. And to revel in the afterglow, wrapped up in the last few notes, before another wave of sound crashed through them again.

When she reached up to take his face in her hands and pull him in for a passionate kiss, he knew she wanted the same thing as he did. Finally, for once, they were on the same page. He held her like the irreplaceable and precious instrument she was. When she invited him in, he entered her slowly, staring deep into her eyes, letting her know he was right there with her, not off in some other place. He needed her to know that he didn't take the gift she was giving him lightly. She was the only thing that mattered in this moment, and all the moments yet to come.

Julia wrapped her legs around him, raising her hips

and pulling him in deeper, and together they found their perfect rhythm. Together, they made their own special song. His eyes never left hers. He wanted to watch the new Julia let go and unfold before him. And when she tensed up and cried out in surprise, gripping his waist harder so she could ride out her wave of pleasure, he covered her mouth with his own, swallowing both their moans as his own pleasure washed through him, carrying him up and up until he floated down like those brilliantly colored leaves.

⚡ ELEVEN

Julia
Six months later

L et's try this again. We have only three weeks and a ton to practice. Ben, you sit next to Julia. She seems to be having trouble with the bridge."

"Mr. G., I know that part really well. I can help her," said Danny, one of three eight-year-olds in the room.

Matthew smiled at Julia. "That's perfect, Danny. Let's rearrange our chairs so that Julia is in the middle of Danny and Ben."

Julia thought there could be nothing worse than taking direction from Matthew, but now she was sandwiched between a teenager and a little kid, both of whom played better than her.

"Don't worry, Homeless, you'll get it. Someday,"

joked Ben. Julia wanted to knock him out with the neck of her guitar, but she just sat and grinned at him. She could do this. She'd dealt with more difficult things and lived.

Like making James partner of her agency. She had doubted her decision right up until they signed the agreement, and even a bit after. Well, a lot after. But after some time, it started to feel like a huge weight had been lifted off of her. She could now focus and pay attention to details she could only rush through before. And now, six months later, she couldn't even imagine how she had run that place on her own. The agency had never had a better quarter, and she knew a lot of that had to do with James. He had her back. They were a team.

Too bad Matthew didn't have her back.

He was throwing her to the wolves.

A concert. In front of everyone. Kate. Andrew. Coop. John. Even her parents. It was going to be a horror show of epic proportions. She had barely managed to play one song, and play it badly. Plus, it was the song Matthew had written for her, and she wanted to do it justice, but man, she sucked. Hard. Sure, Matthew praised her and told her she was getting better, but it was hard not to notice the pained look on his face when she played, especially during the bridge.

It was official. She would go down in history as the one student he simply could not teach. But that didn't stop him. He refused to give up on her, insisting she perform at the year-end concert with the rest of his students. If she didn't, he was going to withhold sex. And grilled cheese. And, well, that was unacceptable. She knew that she could never, ever go without either one again.

So here she sat, among a group of students and her teacher, all of them younger than her and kicking her ass at guitar. She marveled at how the eight-year-olds could pluck their way through a song like it was second nature, while she had barely made friends with CAGED. Even Ben sounded amazing. She really hoped Amy was going to be there to hear him.

"I want us to start at the beginning and play it all the way through. No stopping. Even if you screw up, just keep going. Remember, I don't want perfect. I just want you to give it your best try. You're going to flub up. But don't let that upset you. The point here is to have fun, right? Alright. A one, two, one, two, three…"

Julia tried her hardest. Really, she did. But her fingers had a mind of their own and decided to play whatever they wanted to. She made up her own chords. Fell behind during the chorus. Even Danny shook his head at her and gave up trying to keep her on track.

She couldn't even keep up with an eight-year-old.

But then the strangest thing happened while she was berating herself. She simply stopped playing and looked around the room. She watched Ben sitting still for once, a look of satisfaction on his face as he made his guitar do exactly what he wanted it to. She smiled proudly at Danny, even though he thought she was an idiot. And she stared at Matthew, her boyfriend and now-roommate, holding Gracie the same way he held her—like a precious thing he wanted to make sing with happiness.

And then she *laughed*. A laugh that started all the

way in her toes, and worked its way up and out through her fingertips, as she plucked and strummed again. And for the first time since this whole thing started, she felt like she was having fun. She didn't even care how she sounded. She gave up trying to control her fingers. She just played the song that Matthew had written for her without judging herself. Without fear.

She played her heart out.

The way Matthew had taught her.

THE END

ABOUT THE AUTHOR

Bobbi Ruggiero is an amateur wine aficionado, semi-professional Duran Duran groupie, and expert stalker of Sting and David Gandy. She also has a writing degree from Emerson College. When she's not chasing boys with guitars around the globe, she enjoys spending time with her very understanding husband, Eric, and their Chihuahua rescue dog, Sandy. Young Teacher is her debut novella. You can find her at bobbiruggiero.com or email at authoressbobbi@gmaildotcom.

30929366R00060

Made in the USA
Middletown, DE
12 April 2016